Why do we have to move?

Written by Joy O'Neill

Illustrated by Lisa Southard

Bright Pen

A Bright Pen Book

Text Copyright © Joy O'Neill 2012

Illustration by © Lisa Southard

British Library Cataloguing Publication Data.
A catalogue record for this book is available from the British Library

ISBN 978-0-7552-1525-6

Authors OnLine Ltd
19 The Cinques
Gamlingay, Sandy
Bedfordshire SG19 3NU
England

This book is also available in e-book format, details of which are available at www.authorsonline.co.uk

For Military Children Everywhere

Hello I'm Grace.

I live in the countryside, near the sea, with my Mum and my Dad and my baby brother George and my fluffy dog Molly.

My Mum is an engineer and she fixes helicopters. Sometimes she has to go away to other places for a long time, which makes me sad because I miss her. My Dad is a nurse and he works in the hospital where baby George was born.

In the summer I go out sailing with my Dad in our little boat.

The air smells salty and the sun shines on the waves and

when I eat my sandwiches the seabirds fly overhead hoping

I'll throw bread to them. Sometimes we see seals and

dolphins as well. We can't take it out in the winter because

the sea is too rough and our boat is too small. Instead we

take Molly for walks on the stormy beach.

Sometimes in the school holidays I go to visit my Granny and Granddad in London. We catch the train and I like to sit by the window so that I can watch the fields and animals and higgidly piggidly cottages and houses rushing by. After a while I start to see big factories and rows and rows of houses and flats and busy roads with cars, lorries and buses. I don't think Molly likes going to London because sometimes when people are rushing around they tread on her tail.

When I'm at home I go to the village school. Mrs White is my teacher and my best friends are Beth and Bobby. Beth lives on a farm with her Mum and Dad and her brothers and sometimes her Mum drives her to school in her tractor. Bobby lives next door to me with his Mum and Dad. His Dad is a sailor and he spends a lot of time away at sea.

One day Mum came home and said, "Guess what I've got some really good news, I've got a new job, a better job."

"That's great," smiled Dad. "Well done. When do you start?"

"In a couple of months," answered Mum, "but there is one thing… it's not here".

"Oh," said Dad and he raised his eyebrows. Mum nodded back.

"What is it?" I felt very confused. "Well Grace it means we will have to move house," said Mum, softly.

"We're moving?" I asked.

"Yes," said Mum.

"Away?" I said.

"Yes," said Dad.

"To a new house?" I asked Mum. By now my tummy had a funny feeling.

"Yes," said Mum.

"To a new school?" I muttered.

"Yes," said Dad.

My face felt red and hot and I started to feel angry.

"Why do we have to move?" I shouted.

That evening I felt sick and I didn't want to eat my dinner and I didn't want a bedtime story.

"Are you alright?" whispered Mum.

"I don't want to move."

Mum stroked my arm, "I'm sorry but we don't have any choice because I have a new job and we have to move. I'm sure it will be fine and besides we'll be closer to visit Granny and Granddad." I didn't sleep very well that night and I had a horrible dream that I was being chased through a house by a big black shadow.

The next morning I rushed to get ready. I just wanted to get to school quick to find Bobby and Beth.

Bobby said, "You'll be ok, I moved when I was little and it was ok."

Beth started to cry and that made me upset. "I don't want to move," I sighed. "I know everyone here and I have lots of friends."

I didn't feel much like doing any work in class that morning and Mrs White came and sat next to me.

"You seem very distracted today Grace, is everything ok?" She said quietly.

"We're moving soon and I don't want to go," I explained.

"Oh I see do you know where you're going?" Mrs White asked. "

No," I snapped.

"Try not to worry I'll speak to Mum or Dad after school," she said.

The next week I got into loads of trouble and Mum was really mad with me.

On Monday I left the front door open and Molly chased the cat next door.

On Tuesday I took baby George's drink because I couldn't find the juice but it made him cry.

On Wednesday Mum said she had to go away but I didn't want her to go so I hid her car keys and she had to call the garage.

On Thursday I was looking for a pencil sharpener and I knocked the flowers over on Mrs White's desk and the water covered her work and Mrs White was very cross.

On Friday I shouted at Beth in the playground because she wouldn't join in with my game.

On Saturday I was bored because Dad had packed some of my books so I drew on my bedroom wall in brightly coloured felt tip pens. Mum had spent the day cleaning and she was really mad.

On Sunday when Dad took me sailing I stood up because I felt wriggly and Dad lost his balance and fell in the sea.

That Sunday afternoon Mum and Dad sat down with me to find out what was wrong.

"Why do we have to move?" I asked.

"You know why," said Mum.

"I don't want to," I cried and tears started to sting my eyes.

"What if my teacher is mean and my new school is scary and all the children are horrible to me!"

"You know, we are really going home," Mum said, "because you were born near there and we moved here when you were two years old and now we're moving back."

"We moved when I was little I didn't remember that. I thought I had always lived here." I said. Mum looked around the room and pulled a photo frame from the sideboard.

"Look at this baby photo of you!" Mum smiled, "Can you see the house is different?"

"Oh, it is!' I'd never noticed that before."

"I've got an idea!" said Dad. "Let's go and visit the area next week and have a look at your new school."

"Great idea," beamed Mum.

The next week we all set off to visit my new school. We left early, just after breakfast but we didn't arrive until after lunch. My new Head teacher was waiting to meet us, she was wearing a bright pink scarf and she had a nice smile, she took us for a tour of the school, I really liked all the pictures in the hall, and then we went to meet my new class. My new teacher is called Mr Miles and as we arrived he was about to take the class outside for PE.

"Hello do you want to come and play tag rugby with us?" he grinned. So I went to join them.

"Hello" said a girl with really long hair "My name is Jasmine and I've just moved here from Cyprus."

In the car on the way home Dad asked, "Was that as bad as you thought? Was your teacher mean and were the other children horrible to you?"

"No, not that bad," I smiled back.

I decided to help out at home by packing my books and toys into boxes ready for the move, all except Blue Bunny who always comes with me in the car. I told the whole class about my new school and the tag rugby. Mrs White helped me make a memory box to take to my new house and all of my friends drew pictures and made cards for me to put in the box. At home Mum and Dad told me all about the removal men and how the van would come to our house and take all of our furniture to our new house.

"Not long until we move now. How are you feeling?" asked Mum.

"A bit nervous and a bit excited," I said.

"Don't worry that's just how I feel," sighed Mum.

The day before the move the removal men came really early.

Mum and Dad were really busy helping them to pack so me,

George and Molly went to spend the day with Bobby and his

Mum. We watched some cartoons and played in the garden

and ate pizza for lunch. That night we all stayed with Bobby

and his Mum. After breakfast we all said goodbye before

getting in the car.

"Bye," shouted Bobby. "Come and stay in the holidays."

"I will and you come and stay with me too," I shouted. "Bye, Bye!"

So off we went and I was sad to be leaving my home and friends

but I was looking forward to going back to my first home.